INSPIRING STORIES

FOR AMAZING GIRLS

A Motivational & Empowering Book about Courage,

Perseverance, Problem-Solving and Friendship

Michelle Weiss

CONTENTS

JOIN OUR FACEBOOK GROUP!

If you want to:

- Discover the **latest releases**
- Be offered the possibility of **reading** every e-book (and for some lucky ones, the paperback!) **in advance for free**
- Share discussions with other members about the adventures and lessons your kids have found in our books
- **Learn about our books in progress** before anyone else, including illustrations, book covers, excerpts and more
- Receive some **free gifts**

And so much more!

Then join our Facebook community for exclusive access and fun surprises!

Scan this QR code to enter our group!

INTRODUCTION

What if I could show you the poster girl for strength?

It's time to flip that front camera open and meet the most confident girl I know.

It's you, my dear.

You probably don't believe me right now, but I know the beautiful, bold girl inside you. This is exactly where we (me and all the girls you'll meet inside this book) come in.

Welcome to an entirely new magical world. A world where brave, kind and intelligent young women like you weave their life stories. These girls have brought to you this collection of short stories to not only entertain you but to inspire you as well. To remind you that you are a strong, confident and incredible girl who can do anything in this life.

As you read on and meet each new girl, you'll see they aren't princesses living in castles. They are heroes who face challenges just like you do. And they are here to show you how like them, you can make your dreams come true.

Hidden between the pages of this book are gems of possibility and diamonds of confidence. They shimmer in the darkest of times and the faintest of light. A constant reminder that you have everything it takes to bring your dreams to life. You can do anything you put your mind to, no matter what.

So, my dear girl, get ready to discover how you can change the ordinary into the extraordinary and flip challenges into opportunities. And throughout it all, I hope you learn only one thing: that you are the most unique and incredible thing on this earth.

With a huge hug and lots of well wishes,

Michelle

STICKS AND STONES

Jimmy was bored. It was Saturday morning, and the July sun was warm and bright. He looked out his bedroom window, but none of the neighborhood kids were around—none, that is, except for Gina. Jimmy liked Gina, but sometimes she was too goody-two-shoes.

Jimmy yawned and walked across the street to see if Gina wanted to play. She was sitting on her porch steps when he approached.

"Hey there, Gina. Do you want to play something?"

"Sure. What?" she said, excited to have someone to play with.

"Dunno." Jimmy shrugged. "We could play catch."

"Great!" Gina jumped up and went into her house to grab a ball. She was happy to have someone to play with too. As the youngest child in the neighborhood, sometimes some of the other kids didn't want her around.

"Go home," they'd say. "You're too little."

"But I'm nine," she'd reply. "I am old enough to play."

It didn't matter what she said or how much she pleaded, they wouldn't let her play.

Jimmy was eleven and sometimes got into trouble for doing silly things. One day, he picked flowers from Mrs. Finch's

8

garden to give to his teacher, and Mrs. Finch was so mad she made Jimmy plant her new flowers.

Jimmy stood when Gina came back outside with a ball.

"Let's go to the backyard," she said. "We'll have lots of room."

Jimmy and Gina tossed the ball back and forth in Gina's backyard for fifteen minutes when Jimmy got bored again.

"I don't want to do this anymore. Let's think of something else," he said. Just then, he spotted a small pile of white stones. "Hey, Gina," he said, pointing. "What are those stones for?"

"Oh, those are for my mom's garden. She plants her flowers and puts them on top of the soil. I guess to look pretty. Those are the leftovers."

"Hmm," Jimmy said. "Did you notice Mrs. O'Connor isn't home? She's probably gone for the day to visit her husband. My mom said he's in a nursing home."

"I know. I miss Mr. O'Connor. I saw him the day Mrs. O'Connor had to take him to the home. He looked so sad."

Jimmy and Gina sat on the lawn, thinking about what to do next. They didn't want to waste a sunny day, but they didn't have many options with no one else around.

Suddenly, Jimmy jumped up. "I've got an idea! Let's throw the stones near Mrs. O'Connor's dog and see if we can make him bark."

Gina stood. "Why would we want to do that? It sounds mean."

"Oh, come on. It will be fun. Those stones are small, and we won't hit him. Let's just make him bark."

"That's not fun, Jimmy. And it's not right."

Gina knew Mrs. O'Connor only tied her dog Smokey outside when she was going to be gone all day. Smokey was a good dog, and he loved kids. Sometimes Mrs. O'Connor would let Gina bring Smokey next door to her house.

Jimmy walked over to the stone pile. "I'll just throw a couple to see if he'll bark."

"No, Jimmy. Don't. It's not a good idea. My mom and dad won't like it, and Mrs. O'Connor won't like it."

"Don't be a baby. I'll just toss a few, and then I'll go over and pick them up."

"But—" Gina sat back down and shook her head. She knew nothing she said would change Jimmy's mind.

The O'Connors were the best next-door neighbors anyone could ask for. Gina liked to help Mrs. O'Connor carry in her groceries, and sometimes she would take Smokey for walks around the block.

"Hey, look," Jimmy called out, holding some small sticks. "I'll toss these near the dog too. Maybe he'll pick them up with his mouth and chew them or move them. Maybe he'll build something." Jimmy laughed.

"Stop it," Gina said, her blonde ponytail swaying as she shook her head. "You leave Smokey alone. Let's go do something else."

"Nope. I'll throw the sticks and stones until that stupid dog barks."

"Why? He's a good dog. Why don't you go home now," Gina urged.

"Nope. And if you want to ever play with me or anyone again, you'll keep your mouth shut."

Gina dropped her head, and a tear rolled down her cheek as Jimmy threw sticks and stones at the neighbor's side yard.

Before long, Jimmy had tossed almost all the stones. Gina knew her mom would be mad.

"Aren't you going to pick them up?" Gina asked Jimmy.

"Nope."

Just then, Mrs. O'Connor returned. She got out of her car and looked at all the sticks and stones near Smokey.

"I'm out of here, Gina. Don't tattle on me, or I'll tell everyone you're a baby tattletale. You gotta protect me."

Jimmy ran home so fast that Gina didn't have a chance to say anything. She went into her house, hoping Mrs. O'Connor wouldn't know how the stones got in her yard.

At dinner, Gina could only pick at her food. She wanted to tell her mom and dad about Jimmy and what happened, but she was too scared. She didn't want to be known as a tattletale and wanted to have friends. She couldn't think about what her life would be like with no one to play with.

"You're not eating much," Gina's mother said with concern. "Are you feeling okay?"

"Yes, Mom. I'm fine. I'm just not too hungry."

"You don't have to eat. You may be excused."

Gina left the table and went to her bedroom. She thought about Jimmy and was mad at herself for not stopping him.

As she stared out the window, her thoughts were interrupted when the doorbell rang. She listened as her mom and another woman spoke. Suddenly, she recognized the voice.

It was Mrs. O'Connor.

"Gina, will you come down here, please," her mother called from the bottom of the staircase.

"Yes, Mom," Gina answered. She walked slowly down the stairs as her mom stood waiting.

"Gina, Mrs. O'Connor is here and would like to have a word with you."

"Yes, Mom," Gina said sheepishly as she followed her mom into the kitchen, where Mrs. O'Connor was seated at the table.

"Hello, Gina. How are you?"

"I'm fine, Mrs. O'Connor. How are you?"

Gina's mom motioned her daughter to take a seat. "Mrs. O'Connor came home from visiting Mr. O'Connor and found my garden stones all over her yard as if someone threw them and tried to hit Smokey with them. She found sticks too. Do you know anything about this?"

"No, Mom. I don't. I'm sorry, Mrs. O'Connor."

"That's fine, child. Do you know if the boy Jimmy, who lives across the street, had anything to do with it?"

Gina remembered what Jimmy said about being a tattletale. "No, I don't."

Gina's mom questioned how someone got into her backyard.

Gina shrugged. "I don't know," she said, her stomach twisting for lying to her mom and neighbor. Her mother excused her from the table. Gina stood, thinking about what she had done. She wanted to tell the truth, but she knew she'd never have anyone to play with again if she did. Jimmy would make sure of it.

As Gina walked away, she heard Mrs. O'Connor say she was going over to speak to Jimmy.

Gina was sure Jimmy would lie too.

It wasn't long before Gina learned Jimmy did lie. But, instead of saying he wasn't in the backyard, he said he was and that Gina had thrown the sticks and stones.

Mrs. O'Connor was again in the kitchen, and Gina sat at the table, this time being questioned about why she lied and why she threw the sticks and stones.

"Why would you do that?" her mother asked. "I am so disappointed that you would do such a thing and more disappointed that you would lie about it. That poor boy Jimmy said he tried many times to stop you. What's gotten into you?"

Tears streamed down Gina's face. "I'm sorry, Mom. I didn't mean to lie."

"Sorry isn't good enough. I want you to go next door, pick up every stone, bring it back where you found it, and pile the sticks to the curb. Your father will take care of them. And Gina, you'll carry the stones in your hands. No bag or bucket. That will give you plenty of time to think about what you did."

"Yes, Mom."

Gina went outside and picked up as many stones as she could fit in her hands, and she walked them to her backyard. Back and

forth she went as Jimmy sat in his kitchen watching her through the window, laughing.

When Gina was finished, she went straight to her bedroom and cried herself to sleep.

The following day, Gina's mom woke her early.

"Get dressed and come have breakfast. You can walk with me to the store and help me carry the groceries home."

"Okay, Mom. I'll be down in a minute."

Gina sat quietly and ate her cereal. When she finished, she went to the bathroom to brush her teeth, and out the door she went with her mom.

They walked down the street and rounded the corner. Mrs. Anderson was sitting on her porch and greeted them.

"Mrs. Hawkins, you should be so proud of Gina. What she did yesterday was so noble."

Gina's mom was confused. "I'm sorry, but I don't know what you're talking about."

"Oh, I thought you knew. I had the baby outside in the playpen, and you know how our backyards join, well, Gina and the boy from across the street... I think Jimmy is his name... were in your backyard, and Jimmy threw stones at Mrs. O'Connor's dog. Gina pleaded with him many times to stop, but he didn't. I think your daughter was crying."

Gina's mom looked down at her daughter. "Is this true?"

Gina nodded.

Mrs. Anderson looked at Gina. "I wish there was something I could have done, but I couldn't leave the baby. So as soon as Mrs. O'Connor arrived home, I called her to let her know what Jimmy had done."

"Thank you for this," Gina's mom said. "I guess Mrs. O'Connor knew who did it before coming to my house."

"I did let her know it was the boy across the street," Mrs. Anderson said.

Gina's mom thanked Mrs. Anderson, and she tugged Gina's hand to start walking.

"You have a lot of explaining to do. First, you lied to Mrs. O'Connor; she must have known you lied. Can you tell me why you lied?"

Gina told her mother the truth—how she tried to stop Jimmy, what he told her would happen if she tattled, and how no one would ever play with her again.

"Let this be a lesson to you, Gina. You will always get caught in a lie, so tell the truth no matter how hard it may seem. You lied to protect Jimmy, and he lied so he wouldn't be in trouble. When we return from the store and put the groceries away, we need to walk across the street and speak with Jimmy's mother."

"Okay," Gina said shyly. "But will I be a tattletale?"

"No, you aren't a tattletale. But you need to apologize to Mrs. O'Connor for lying to her, and I think Jimmy needs to apologize to you both. I hope this has taught you that honesty is always the best policy."

CROSS MY HEART

Lively Benson was most at home at a dance studio. The jazz classes at a local dance studio were the highlight of each week, and she was always sad when the season ended. Sensing her passion and dedication, her parents converted their basement into a home studio with mirrored walls and floor mats to allow her to continue dancing all year. And dance she did! Lively spent all her free time in that studio. She felt safe there.

Like most new parents, when Lively was born, her mom and dad counted her fingers and toes. Ten little toes. Five little fingers on the right hand. But her left hand was different. Lively was born with a birth defect that affected her left hand. She was missing three fingers, and the two present were shorter than average. The condition had a long, tongue-twisting name that was difficult to pronounce, so Lively never tried.

Lively did not let her hand stop her from doing anything. Not only did she dance, but she played basketball and ran track at her middle school. When kids would ask her what was wrong with her hand, she would reply nothing was wrong. She was born how she was meant to be. Most kids her age were understanding when she explained. They would shrug their shoulders and say, "Okay. Whatever," before moving to the next topic.

But there was one person who would not move on: Ava Brown. The best dancer in the studio, she was also the prettiest and the most popular. The dance instructors fawned over her. Lively was able to avoid Ava at the studio during the season because they were in different classes. However, the off-season was a different story. Their parents were friends and liked to barbecue and have pool parties together. They took turns hosting and were together nearly every weekend.

School was out for the summer, and the end-of-the-season recital had wrapped up a week ago. Lively was missing the studio already.

"Mom, could we look for a dance class that I could take over the summer?" she asked as she watched her mother fold pool towels fresh from the dryer.

"Honey, you know that your father and I would if we could, but it just isn't in the cards with work and the cost." Her mother ran her fingers through Lively's thick brown hair.

Lively shooed her away. "You're going to mess up my hair." Lively had recently taken to styling her hair and wearing mascara.

"If it helps, your father can repaint your studio and freshen the mats. We have the budget for that."

Lively rolled her eyes and sighed. It was not the answer she was looking for. It was not a bad idea; the light pink paint looked babyish.

"Where is Dad? I want to ask him when he can start." Lively jumped from one foot to the next, raising her arms slowly from her sides up above her head while wiggling her fingers.

Her mother laughed. "You never stop dancing, do you?"

"Nope." Lively spun around on her toes, making a dramatic leap out of the laundry room toward the kitchen.

"Your father is outside cleaning the grill. The Browns are coming over for barbecue ribs. I've made a ton of food, so please don't ruin your supper with snacks."

Lively's excitement faded quickly when she realized that having Mr. and Mrs. Brown over for supper meant that Ava would also be coming.

"You can bring Ava down to your studio. Brainstorm ideas for paint colors," her mom said hesitantly. Her mom knew that Lively and Ava did not get along.

"You two could be good for each other. I wish you both would try." Lively followed her mother to the patio, simmering at the thought of bringing Ava into her studio.

"She makes fun of me, Mom. She makes fun of my hand. I don't want to be made fun of."

"I am sorry she makes fun of you. That's not nice. But I want you to try to put yourself in her shoes."

"What does that mean? You want me to try her shoes on?" Lively was confused.

"No, silly girl. I want you to imagine how you would feel if you were in her situation."

Lively was even more confused. What situation? Ava was the best dancer, and she was the most popular. She had all the best clothes and shoes. Being in her shoes seemed like it would make Lively happy. It did not explain why Ava made fun of her.

"Lively, all I want you to do is talk to her for a bit. Show her your studio and talk about dance. Listen to her. That is all I ask. Can you do that for me?"

"I'm hungry. A snack would help me think it over," Lively negotiated.

"One snack. That is it." Her mother ran her fingers through Lively's hair again.

"Mom!" Lively ducked away back into the kitchen. She grabbed a granola bar and retreated to the front porch.

Lively sat down in the big brown rocking chair. Her dad said this was a good thinking chair. Pointing her toes until her feet were fully extended, she barely tapped the surface of the porch. The rocker gently motioned backward and forward.

Lively thought about how she could approach Ava.

"Hey, Ava!"

"What's up, Ava?"

"Fine weather we have today, isn't it?"

Lively rehearsed aloud, but nothing felt right. What did her mother mean that not everything is what it seems on the outside? Why do parents have to be so cryptic? The thinking chair was not helping.

Before Lively could decide her approach, a sparkling black Range Rover pulled up in front of her house. Lively's stomach dropped. The Browns had arrived.

Mr. Brown held the door while Ava exited the vehicle like an actor stepping onto the red carpet.

"Hi, Lively!" The Browns were exuberant people, always beaming with happiness.

"Your mom tells me that you and Ava will be spending time in your studio. I am so happy. You girls can learn a lot from each other," Mrs. Brown said. She kissed Ava on top of the head, and

Mr. and Mrs. Brown skip-walked up the sidewalk and into the house.

Lively looked at Ava, who was frowning. Unlike her parents, Ava always looked sad, angry, or bored.

Ava looked at her nails, which she had bitten down to the nubs of her fingers.

"My parents have been talking all week about how much we can learn from each other. I have no idea what they are talking about." Ava rolled her eyes. "I swear they are speaking in code."

A nervous laugh escaped Lively. "I feel the same way. My mom has been talking like that all day. I'm so confused." Lively rubbed her left hand with her right hand. Lively hated that she had a nervous tic that drew attention to the one part about herself that she did not want people to notice.

"I don't know what I could learn from you. I am not like you at all. I have two whole hands." Ava stomped by Lively, waving her hands in front of Lively's face. Lively followed behind her. She was feeling angry now.

"Ava, you are not nice to me, and I will not listen to it. I am *not* going to bring you into my studio. You don't deserve to be there!" Lively was yelling now, tears forming in her eyes.

Ava stopped on the balls of her feet and slowly turned around. Lively could not believe what she was seeing. There were tears in Ava's eyes also. Instead of feeling bad for Ava, Lively felt even more angry.

"What do you have to cry about, little Miss Perfect? You have two whole hands. Awesome clothes. Your parents are rich and have a fancy truck. The dance instructors think you're the greatest dancer ever!" Lively was shaking, and the tears were streaming down her face.

Ava was crying now. "They only talk to me because of who my parents are. They don't care about me. My mom was a ballet dancer and a real stage ballerina. Our dance instructors want my mom to teach at the studio. And my dad, well, you are right. He is rich. The studio owner is always asking him for donations."

Lively could not believe what came out of her mouth next.

"I am sorry they treat you that way. That isn't nice at all."

Ava's mouth dropped open slightly. "What?"

"I am sorry. I would feel so, so… mad. And sad. I think." Lively had only thought of how good she would feel if the instructors showed her the kind of attention they gave Ava. Now that she knew the attention was fake and for all the wrong reasons, Lively could imagine Ava's anger and sadness when she was in the studio.

Ava wiped her face with the backs of her hands. "I just want them to leave me alone. Let me dance. That's how they treat you. I am jealous of you because of that."

"Wow." Lively could not think of anything better to say.

The two girls stood silently, Lively rubbing her left hand and Ava biting her nails and sniffling.

Ava broke the silence. "I'm sorry I said that about having two hands. That was so mean." Ava's face turned red, and the tears started to flow again.

"If you promise you won't say stuff like that anymore, I promise you can come into my studio whenever you want." Again, Lively could not believe what was coming out of her mouth.

"I promise. Cross my heart." Ava crossed her fingers over her heart and extended her hand to Lively. "Friends?"

Lively crossed her fingers over her heart and took Ava's hand with a big smile. "Friends."

SPREAD YOUR WINGS

Lauren Oliver loved books. She loved the smell of the cover and the feel of the paper. But, more than that, she loved the words on the pages. Her favorite word was hippopotamus. She thought it was fun to say and spell.

Lauren spent a lot of time reading. She was shy and didn't have many friends. Books were her friends.

At school, she often sat alone at lunch. She wanted to sit with others but was too shy to start a conversation. She had one friend, Darlene, whom she met at the ice skating rink last year, but Darlene went to a different school. At least they got to talk on the phone, and sometimes, they would go to each other's houses on the weekends.

Lauren was nervous because her teacher, Mr. Rose, gave her a sealed envelope to take home to her mother. She had no idea what it could be about. Her grades were good; in fact, they were excellent. She never got in trouble, was polite, and always used her manners.

When the school day ended, Lauren ran home as fast as she could. She wanted to know what was inside the mysterious envelope.

"Lauren, you've qualified for the school's spelling bee. The winner will go on to the state finals," her mother said, holding the letter for Lauren to see. "This is such an honor. I'm so proud of you."

Lauren looked at the letter, then at her mom.

"Mom, you know I can't do it. I can't get up in front of a lot of people. I wouldn't be able to even think of how to spell the word spell!"

"Nonsense, child. You can do it. This is an honor to be chosen. Don't let your shyness stop you from something so wonderful."

"I can't do it, Mom. I'm so sorry."

Lauren ran to her room, tears streaming from her eyes. She knew she was disappointing her mother, and she knew when her dad got home and learned she didn't want to be in the spelling bee, he'd be disappointed, too. After all, he'd told Lauren many times how he won the state spelling bee championship in sixth grade. Lauren was in fourth grade, but she knew words that many of her classmates didn't.

Lauren dried her eyes and telephoned Darlene.

"Do it!" Darlene shouted with excitement. "You need to do this, Lauren. It's an honor to be selected."

Lauren sighed. "That's what my mom said. I'm sure half of the school was picked. It's no big deal."

"You spell better than anybody I know. You can win. I know you can."

Darlene's excitement and encouragement didn't change Lauren's mind. She knew she'd freeze on a stage with the audience staring and judges watching her every move.

No, it was something she couldn't do.

Lauren went to school the following day prepared to tell Mr. Rose that she wasn't interested in participating in the spelling bee but appreciated the offer. Before she could say anything, Mr. Rose told her she'd be practicing after school with Jenny White.

"I called your mother to let her know you'll be in the school library after school for the next two weeks. She'll be picking you up. You'll leave at the side door by the gym as the main doors will be locked," Mr. Rose said.

Jenny White, Lauren thought. She was just as shy as Lauren. How could two shy girls practice together?

"Hey there, Lauren. It's great to see you," Jenny greeted as she sat across from Lauren. "I'm happy I was chosen to practice with you?"

Lauren froze, staring at Jenny. This wasn't the same Jenny she knew. Even though she hadn't seen Jenny this school year because they weren't in the same class, she remembered how quiet and shy she was just last year.

"Lauren, are you okay?" Jenny asked.

"I-I, well, yes," Lauren answered quietly. "We should get started."

Jenny and Lauren went back and forth, spelling the words on Mr. Rose's list.

Lauren said the first word, and Jenny spelled it out. They took turns until they got to the last word. They did this every school day until the day of the spelling bee. But each day, Lauren and Jenny talked more and more. They talked about their favorite television shows and books and how much they love to ice skate.

"Can you go skating on Saturday afternoon? My mom can bring us and pick us up?" Jenny asked Lauren.

"I'll ask my mom. I'm sure she'll say yes."

"Great, here's my number. Call me tonight after you ask," Jenny said, handing Lauren a paper with her number.

When Lauren got home, she ran to the kitchen to ask her mom about skating with Jenny.

"Of course, you can go. I'll just need to speak to Jenny's mom before you go," Lauren's mom said, surprised by the request. "Lauren, I'm a little confused. How did this come about?"

"Jenny asked me," she said. "We both love to skate."

Lauren's mom smiled. Could it be her daughter was getting over her shyness?

Lauren couldn't wait for Saturday. She and Jenny planned to meet Darlene at the ice rink. When Jenny's mom arrived, Lauren was already outside waiting.

The three girls spent the afternoon skating, laughing, and trying not to fall. When the session ended, they got hot chocolate and sat at a table, waiting for Jenny's mom to pick them up.

"I'm so happy for you," Darlene said to Lauren. "How did you do it?"

"Do what?" Lauren asked.

"Make a new friend, and stop being so shy," Darlene answered.

"It just happened. We practiced together for the spelling bee and just started talking about other things."

"See how easy it is?" Jenny said. "That's how I did it. You just have to let it happen. Start a conversation with someone, and you'll see how you have things in common."

"I never thought I could talk to anyone," Lauren said.

"But you did," Jenny said excitedly. "And now you have a new friend, and I have two." She looked at Darlene. "I'm so happy you came today."

The trio vowed to spend more time together, and Lauren and Jenny rode to the spelling bee with Jenny's mom, picking up Darlene along the way to the school. Lauren's mom and dad rode with Jenny's dad. Not only did the girls become friends, but so did their parents.

Lauren's stomach felt like a big knot when they arrived, and her palms were sweaty. She was nervous but not scared to talk with other contestants while waiting her turn.

Finally, her name was called. She walked to the microphone and looked out to the audience. Her mom and dad were smiling, and so were Jenny's parents. Darlene gave her a thumbs-up as the judge announced the word Lauren was to spell: hippopotamus.

   This was going to be a piece of cake.

NOTHING CAN STOP ME NOW

Every school day at recess, Eliza watched from her wheelchair as her classmates played on the playground. They would swing or teeter-totter, and others would round up enough players for a kickball game.

Eliza wanted nothing more than to join them. She tried to run and play like her classmates. Although she knew that she would never run, she wanted to play. She didn't understand why she couldn't swing or teeter-totter, but she knew she couldn't get out of her wheelchair without help, and her teacher didn't have the support needed to assist Eliza.

"Do you want to be in the sun or shade today?" her teacher, Mrs. Stone, would ask every day.

"The sun is fine," Eliza would answer each time. She didn't like being in the shade. She liked to feel the warmth on her skin. It was the only highlight of recess.

In the classroom, Eliza could do almost everything her classmates did. Because her wheelchair was larger than the desk chairs, she sat at a special table made to accommodate a wheelchair.

Eliza couldn't play gym like the others, but Mrs. Finch, the gym teacher, included Eliza as often as possible. Eliza could play catch and some of the other games. Mrs. Finch picked activities that Eliza could participate in as often as possible.

Sometimes, it just wasn't possible, and Eliza sat on the sidelines watching.

Eliza had a lot of friends, but none knew how sad she felt because she couldn't play at recess. She didn't want to tell anyone, not even her best friend Casey. Eliza didn't want anyone to feel sorry for her. She liked that the rest of her classmates treated her like everyone else and didn't want anyone to feel sorry for her.

Sometimes, Casey would ask her questions about not being able to run like the others, and Eliza always answered that it didn't bother her. She did like it when winter came, and recess was held inside, usually playing board games or reading. Eliza's favorite indoor recess was when the girls would sit together and talk. She thought it was nice they could do that. Some kids, like Jason Peterson, would fall asleep in the beanbag chair and snore. The girls would giggle and talk about ways to wake him, but they knew they wouldn't try. It was fun coming up with ways, though.

Every day at lunchtime, Eliza's classmates took turns wheeling her to the cafeteria. Her wheelchair was electric, and she could get herself there, but her classmates enjoyed pushing her there and back.

Sometimes, one of her classmates would ask Eliza why she couldn't walk. She would explain the car accident she was in and how she remembers running and playing with other kids.

"I have walked before, and I could run," she'd say when asked. "But after the accident, I couldn't move my legs like I used to. I can still move them a little, but it's okay because I am happy my mom, dad, and brother didn't get hurt. I would be sad if they were."

Eliza vowed never to let her sadness show. As much as she tried to hide it, Casey saw it. She saw it every time Eliza watched the class play at recess, which bothered her.

"I'll sit with you," Casey offered every day, and every day, Eliza refused.

"I'm fine. Play with the others. I like watching when you play kickball and get out," Eliza said with a laugh. "You crack me up."

"Ha, ha," Casey said as she ran off. "Nobody will get me out today!"

Suddenly, Eliza wasn't coming to school. She was absent for an entire week, then another and another. Casey would call Eliza's house, but no one ever answered. Mrs. Stone would know, but she only announced to the class that Eliza would not be attending for a long time.

Two months passed, and Eliza was still not in school. Casey and the others figured she and her family must have moved away, and Eliza left without saying goodbye.

Then, three months later, the class went outside for recess on a warm, sunny day. They were playing kickball when someone called out to them.

"Hey, do you need a pinch-kicker?"

The game stopped as everyone turned to see who it was.

"Eliza!" a chorus rang out. "Is that really you, Eliza?"

The classmates ran over to her.

"What?"

"How?"

"For real?"

A flood of questions came pouring out of their mouths.

Eliza flashed a broad smile.

"I went to a hospital in Boston and had two surgeries to repair my legs," she explained. "I only need these crutches now; soon, I might not need them. I am having a lot of therapy and can kick a ball. I can't run yet, but I am doing my best to get so I can."

Eliza told her classmates that not everyone can have surgeries to help them walk again, but her injury was eligible for the surgery and worth trying. Fortunately, it worked for her.

"It doesn't work for everyone, but technology is making a lot of advances, so people can do more if they are in a wheelchair. So, let's get this game going again!"

As everyone cheered, Casey helped Eliza walk to the kickball field.

"You can kick for me," she said as they reached the field. "I am up now, so let's see what you can do."

With Casey's help, Eliza stepped to the plate. Bobby Bonnell pitched the ball, and Eliza kicked a grounder to third base. Casey ran and made it to first base.

"Great kick," Casey yelled.

"Nothing can stop me now!" Eliza answered as she prepared to kick for Sarah DuBois. "Nothing at all!"

THE BIG SURPRISE

Eva hurried to school Monday morning to try out for the school play. The tryouts were held before classes started, so Eva needed to wake up earlier than usual. She didn't mind. She wanted nothing more than to win a part in "The Wizard of Oz."

She walked into the auditorium and looked around until she found her friend Paloma.

"I'll never get a part," Eva said. "Look how many are here."

Paloma agreed. "How will we all get to try out before classes start?"

"I don't know, but we'll soon find out," Eva said.

Mr. Zollo entered the stage and walked to the podium. He tapped the microphone a few times to make sure it was on.

"Ladies and gentlemen, we have a great crowd here today, which pleases me," Mr. Zollo announced. "Because there are more than expected, you'll be trying out in pairs. Be prepared to come to the stage quickly when I call your name. I assume you've all practiced the lines I handed out last week. As you'll be in pairs, feel free to ad-lib if you don't want to read the same lines as your partner."

Eva turned to Paloma and whispered, "I hope we go last to see how the others do."

"Me too. We're supposed to sit in the cafeteria when we're done, and that's so boring."

Their hope of being last was shattered when Mr. Zollo called them to be first.

"Eva and Paloma, please come to the stage. As you both have been in plays before, you can show the others how a tryout should go. We have many new faces here today."

Eva read the prepared lines, and Paloma ad-libbed. When they finished, Mr. Zollo announced that they gave a remarkable performance, and that's how a tryout should be done.

"Don't simply read the lines; show movement and facial expressions. Thank you, Eva and Paloma. You can go to the cafeteria now."

Paloma looped her arm through Eva's. "Maybe we'll get a part. He did use us as an example," she said.

"I sure hope so. It would make sitting in the cafeteria for thirty minutes worthwhile." Eva laughed. "We should find out tomorrow if we got a part."

"I know you will. I'm not so sure about if I will."

"Oh, Paloma. You'll get a part. You're so good!"

The wait to learn who got a part didn't take long. Eva and Paloma were called to the auditorium after school.

"Everyone, when I call you, please come to the stage to pick up the script. Your lines are highlighted in yellow. Please study them and be prepared to begin practice after school each day for the next three weeks. Make sure your parents know you'll be staying, and a late bus will be provided," Mr. Zollo said. "You can ride the late bus even if you normally walk."

Eva took Paloma's hand as they waited. "Good luck," she whispered. "I'm so nervous.

"Paloma, please come to the stage."

Eva watched as Paloma approached Mr. Zollo.

"Will you accept the role of Dorothy?" Mr. Zollo asked Paloma.

She squealed, and everyone clapped. With a huge smile, Paloma walked off the stage with her script.

Mr. Zollo announced the wizard, scarecrow, lion, and Tin Man, then called Eva to the stage.

"Will you accept the role of the good witch?" he asked Eva.

"Yes, yes!" she said. "I would be honored."

With scripts in hand, Eva and Paloma walked home together. Eva couldn't wait to tell her mother and father. She was so happy to be playing the good witch. She was happy, too, that Paloma got the female lead.

Paloma was excited, but she was also sad. Her father couldn't attend the play because he was deployed overseas, serving his country in the Marines. He wasn't due home until the school year ended—too late for him to see the play. Still, she was happy that Mr. Zollo said he would try to arrange for Paloma's father to watch it on a video call, and it would be recorded so he could watch it later.

For the next three weeks, Eva and Paloma practiced, and as the big opening night was days away, Paloma grew sadder.

"My dad won't get to see me," she told Eva. "The yellow brick road is too far away."

Eva put her arm around Paloma. "I know it's not easy. I'd want my dad here too, and he will be for both of us."

"I know," Paloma said. "My dad is doing good things, and I know he'd be here if he could."

The big night came, and Mr. Zollo stood at the podium to address the audience.

"As we present to you our play, it is a reminder that when we follow the right road, we can meet the man behind the curtain. Tonight, you'll meet the man behind the curtain thanks to one student with a kind heart, a great idea, and the courage to seek help. Please welcome Dorothy and the good witch."

"What's he doing?" Paloma asked as they walked onto the stage from the room to the left.

Eva shrugged. "Who knows."

"Ladies and gentlemen, we have a little preview tonight for you. You all know how the play ends. The man behind the curtain is exposed. Tonight, we're going to do something different. Tonight, we're going to begin the play at the end," Mr. Zollo announced.

Sighs and gasps of confusion filled the auditorium.

"Dorothy, would you do the honor of pulling the curtain open."

"Sure, I guess," Paloma answered, confused by the strange request.

Paloma pulled the cord, and the curtain opened. She let out a scream and started crying. There stood her dad in full uniform, smiling with open arms. She ran to him and hugged him so hard he almost fell over.

"I can't believe this! How did you get here... I mean, how were you able?" Paloma asked through happy tears.

"Your friend Eva. Her dad works for the government in defense," her father said, hugging her again. "Now, I'm going to sit in the audience with your mother and watch my daughter give the performance of a lifetime."

Paloma's father gave his daughter one more hug before exiting the stage.

Paloma scanned the stage for Eva, and when she saw her off to the side, she walked over and hugged her.

"How did you get my dad here?" Paloma asked, still crying happy tears.

"We'll talk after the play," Eva said.

Mr. Zollo introduced the cast, and they received a standing ovation at the end.

"Before everyone leaves, I'd like to thank Eva Williamson for the compassion and kindness she showed her friend Paloma. Sergeant Major Gregory Marshall would like to come to the stage now."

Loud applause broke out as Paloma's father walked to the stage. He presented Eva with a dozen red roses.

"Thank you, Eva, for ensuring I arrived tonight and convincing your dad to get me a three-day pass. It means the world to me," he said.

The audience roared with applause as Paloma and her father walked off the stage.

"This has been the best day of my life," Paloma said.

Her father took her hand. "And there will be many, many more."

DON'T JUMP TO CONCLUSIONS

Gabrielle looked over at the empty seat in her math class.

"Again?" she said to Ace, who sat behind her. "Why is Danelle always absent? Do you think she moved to another school?"

"She must have," Ace said. "It's kind of weird that nobody's said anything. It's like she's disappeared."

"I hope she isn't sick," Gabrielle said as Miss Potter told her to turn around.

Gabrielle and Danelle had been good friends since first grade. Their teacher called them the "Double Elles," and they would giggle. By the time they reached fifth grade, the nicknames had stuck, and they were known as the "Double Elles" to almost everyone in the school.

Because Gabrielle and Danelle were such good friends, their classmates assumed Gabrielle knew why Danelle hadn't been in school. The more time that passed, the more Gabrielle was asked. Yet, she asked others, including Ace, who was also a good friend of Danelle's, had no idea why.

Danelle was at school one day and gone the next, and the next, and the next. Gabrielle was concerned because she hadn't heard from Danelle, not even a phone call or text message.

The days passed with the seat staying empty in math class. During lunch in the cafeteria, everyone started talking about the mysterious absence.

"My mother said she and her family left town," Sandy Blake said. "My mother knows someone whose cousin sold their house and said they moved a month ago."

"That's not true," Jose Padula said. "Danelle's mom shops at my dad's store all the time. She was just there the other day."

"Have your dad ask why Gabrielle hasn't been in school," MaryKate Andrews said. "That's easy enough."

"I'm not going to do that," Jose said. "It's not my business, and it's not anyone's business. If she wanted us to know why she's not here, don't you think she'd tell one of us?"

"Maybe she can't. Maybe she can't talk," MaryKate said. "I heard she can't talk."

"Who told you that?" Gabrielle asked MaryKate.

"I can't tell. It's a secret."

The next day, everyone talked about Danelle and how she could not speak. Some kids said she had an accident, and others said she was sick and couldn't talk.

Gabrielle didn't believe any of it. She didn't like the rumors that were spread about her friend.

"Ace, did you hear anything about Danelle?" she turned around and asked before math class started.

"I heard a few things about her being sick and being in a boating accident," Ace answered. "I don't think any of it's true. I think it's strange that she's not here, and we don't know why, but I'm sure we'll find out sooner or later."

Gabrielle couldn't concentrate on her math lesson. She wondered how Danelle was keeping up with schoolwork if she wasn't coming to school. Missing a lot of lessons would be hard to catch up because they've been learning a lot. Soon, it would be time for final exams and the end of the school year. Gabrielle hoped Danelle would be back before school ended. If not, she might never see her again, especially if it's true that she moved away.

More days passed, which meant more rumors about why Danelle wasn't in school. Sandy insisted Danelle and her family

sold their house and moved out of town. MaryKate insisted Danelle was unable to speak and would never return to school.

Neither Ace nor Jose wanted any part of the rumors, nor did Gabrielle. She wanted to know why her friend wasn't coming to school and if she was okay.

"Is her mom still going to your dad's store?" she asked Jose.

"Yes, my dad said she was there yesterday," he said. "She hasn't moved. MaryKate is making that up."

"But why would she do that?" Ace asked.

"I think everybody just wants to know where Danelle is and why she isn't coming to school," Jose answered.

Gabrielle sighed. "She hasn't been here in five or six weeks, and she hasn't tried to get ahold of me."

"I'm sure the principal knows why she's not here," Ace said. "And probably the teachers."

"Yeah, everybody but us," Gabrielle said.

Later that day, Gabrielle was sitting at the dinner table with her family when her cell phone rang.

"Mother, may I see who it is?" she asked.

"You may be excused," her mother said as Gabrielle jumped from her seat and ran to the living room to get her phone.

"Mom, mom, it was Danelle. I missed her call."

"Well, call her back," Gabrielle's mother said, happy her daughter had finally heard from her friend.

Gabrielle rushed to her bedroom and called Danelle. She was thrilled when she heard her answer.

"Where are you? Where have you been? Why aren't you in school?" Gabrielle asked in rapid succession.

"Slow down, Elle," Danelle said and laughed. "I'll explain if you give me a chance."

"Tell me, tell me. I've been so worried."

Danelle explained how she had fallen in the bathtub and broken her leg in three places. She needed special surgery, so she had to go out of town to a bigger hospital where a surgeon knew how to fix her leg.

"I was in a big cast for six weeks, and my leg was elevated. When the cast came off, I had to have therapy to learn how to use it again. I couldn't call you, Gabrielle. I am so sorry. I didn't have my cell phone with me, and I didn't have a phone in my room. I wouldn't have been able to reach it, anyway," Danelle said.

"Oh, that sounds so painful. Are you okay now?" Gabrielle asked.

"It hurt, but the doctors made me all better, and I can walk now. I have a scar. I'll show it to you at school tomorrow."

"You're coming to school tomorrow?" Gabrielle was so excited. It was the best news she had all week.

"I'll be there, and I can't wait to see you and Ace."

"How did you keep up with schoolwork?" Gabrielle asked.

Danelle explained she had a tutor who came to the hospital three times a week and got all the work from her teachers every Friday.

"They emailed my tutor everything you were working on, and I did my work and emailed it."

Gabrielle couldn't wait to get to school the next morning. She skipped breakfast and hurried out the door. She hugged Danelle when she saw her, and they walked to math together.

Miss Potter welcomed Danelle back to school.

"Class, you've all missed Danelle, and so have I," Miss Potter said. "I also heard all the rumors going around the school, and I hope you all learn a lesson that you shouldn't jump to conclusions. Know the facts before you say anything about anybody or any situation."

MaryKate and Sandy apologized to Danelle at lunch for jumping to conclusions and spreading rumors.

64

"Jumping to conclusions isn't good," Danelle said. "And neither is jumping out of the bathtub to answer your cell phone."

MaryKate, Sandy, Ace, and Jose couldn't wait to hear the rest of the real story.

SYLVIA'S WISH

Sylvia was happy that she would spend two weeks of summer vacation at her Aunt Louise's. Her aunt lived in a small town three hours away from Sylvia's home. Not only did Sylvia like getting away from the big city where she lived, but her aunt's neighborhood had a lot of kids her age who looked forward to her visit each summer.

Sylvia was treated special by the neighborhood kids. They would gather every morning at her aunt's to play together.

And play they did, from early morning until it was time for supper. They would barely break for lunch and sometimes eat together at Aunt Louise's picnic table.

Sylvia had a lot of friends when she visited her aunt, a lot more than she did at home. She enjoyed every minute of her vacation, but it was hard to leave when the two weeks had passed.

"She's here, she's here," Kota, Beth, Dayton, Josie, Anton, and Roger shouted when Sylvia got out of her mother's car. The friends gathered around Sylvia as she hugged each one.

"I've got to unpack and talk to Aunt Louise. I'll come play later," Sylvia said.

She went inside and, after a lovely chat with her aunt, Sylvia went outside to be with her friends. They played all kinds of games until it was time to go home.

Aunt Louise smiled when Sylvia walked through the door. She was covered in dirt and grass stains, a sign of a fun time.

"Hop right in the tub, young lady, and I'll fix you a bedtime snack. Bring me your clothes so I can wash them."

Sylvia took her bath and got ready for bed. She went to the living room to say goodnight to her aunt.

"I had so much fun here, Aunt Louise," she said, sitting beside her on the couch. "I wish I could stay here forever. I wish I had this many friends back home."

"Do you try to make friends?" Aunt Louise asked.

"Not really. It's different in the city. The kids I go to school with live too far away to play. Can I live here forever?"

Aunt Lousie chuckled. "I don't think you'd like living here all the time. Josie and Anton are like you. They don't live here. They come to stay with their father for the summer. Kota and Beth live here, but I don't see them outside much once school

68

starts, and Roger is homeschooled, so he's inside most days. Dayton plays sports, so he's very busy."

"But I don't have friends to play with when I go home. I have a few school friends, but we never get together after school."

"You don't have any friends at all close by?"

"No, Aunt Louise. That's why I love coming here every summer. Well, I love coming to see you, too!"

"We can talk more in the kitchen. I've made you popcorn," Aunt Louise said, waving her hand for Sylvia to join her.

"Are you sure I can't live here?" Sylvia pleaded.

"Sylvia, I would love to have you, but I'm afraid I could not take care of a ten-year-old, and your parents would miss you. And what about your dog Sallie?"

"Sallie could move here with me," Sylvia answered.

"I'm afraid I can't have a dog in the house. I sneeze when I'm around pets. That's why I don't have any."

Sylvia understood, kissed her aunt goodnight, and went to her room. She loved that Aunt Lousie kept it special just for her. It was painted in her favorite color—pink—and she had toys, games, and puzzles. Aunt Louise kept the room just for Sylvia. She promised no one else would sleep there.

The following day, the gang came to the door early, and Aunt Louise invited them in for pancakes and eggs. Sylvia poured them orange juice, saying, "I wish I could do this every day for the rest of my life."

"Me too," Kota said. "I wish you were here all the time."

The others agreed. Sylvia smiled. She was so happy to have so many friends but wished she never had to leave.

The days passed, and Sylvia enjoyed playing with her summer friends. They played games, swam in Roger's pool, and went to the playground a block away. Aunt Louise let them go without her, knowing the park was supervised.

One morning, Aunt Louise invited all the children in for breakfast. She told them she had an idea.

"When you go home for dinner, ask if you can come back, and we will go outside to catch fireflies and play some games in the dark. This is Sylvia's last night here, and I'd like to make it special," Aunt Louise said.

"It's my last night?" Sylvia asked. A tear rolled down her cheek. "Already?"

"I'm sorry, dear. Your mother and father are coming to get you tomorrow. They miss you."

"I miss them, too. But I'm going to miss my friends. I wish I could stay longer."

"I know, dear," Aunt Louise said. "Now, let's eat so you can get outside to play."

When breakfast was finished, the children helped Aunt Louise clear the table and then rushed outside to start a game of tag. Later, they would go swimming in Roger's pool. His mother invited all the kids to an afternoon of swimming and lemonade. Sylvia thought it was a wonderful way to spend her final day with her friends.

After dinner, everyone gathered at Aunt Louise's. She handed out jars and led them to her backyard to catch fireflies. They ran around and chased the bugs as their light blinked.

"This is so much fun," Josie said. "I wish I could do this every night."

"I do, too!" Beth said as she caught her first firefly.

"When we've finished, we are releasing the fireflies," Aunt Louise said. "That's why there are holes in the jar lids. The fireflies can breathe until we let them go."

"This is great!" Kota squealed. "The fireflies look so cool in the jar when they light up. This was the best idea ever!"

Aunt Louise told them to count their fireflies and release them. Kota was excited as he caught the most.

When everyone released their fireflies, they played a game of tag with flashlights that Aunt Louise brought out.

The children played until nine-thirty, and Aunt Louise walked each one home.

Sylvia hugged them goodbye and cried as she returned to the house with Aunt Louise.

"I wish I could stay another week, please, please," Sylvia begged.

"I'm sorry, dear. I know how much fun you have when you're here, and I love having you." Aunt Louise took Sylvia's hand. "It's such a beautiful night. Shall we take some ice cream from the freezer and enjoy it on the porch?"

"Sure," Sylvia said, her head hung low.

Aunt and niece ate ice cream, and Sylvia looked up to the sky and wished upon a star.

"Star light, star bright, please grant me my wish tonight."

"Sylvia, I know you wish you could stay, but sometimes, we can't always get what we wish for, and we need to be grateful for what we have."

"I know, Auntie, but I get bored at home. Here, I have friends. And I don't get to see them or talk to them until I return next summer," Sylvia pouted.

Aunt Louise perked up. "I have an idea. I will give you envelopes with stamps with all your friends' addresses, and I'll do the same for them with your address."

"Really? Do you think they will write to me?" Sylvia asked excitedly.

"I'm sure they will. I'll remind them if you don't hear from them, but it's an excellent way to keep in touch."

Sylvia kissed her aunt goodnight and went to her room. She tried to fall asleep, but all she could think about was leaving. Finally, she gave in and fell fast asleep.

When she woke the next morning, she was surprised to see her friends at the breakfast table.

"We're having an envelope exchange!" Beth said. "We're going to write you letters, and you better answer back!"

"I will," Sylvia said. She turned to Aunt Louise. "I am so grateful you did this for me, and I'm grateful even though I didn't get my wish. I got something just as good—keeping up with my friends all year."

AVERIE'S PERSEVERANCE

Averie did not want to go inside the school. She didn't know anyone, and her English wasn't very good. She missed her hometown of Montreal and her friends.

Averie had to move to the United States because her father accepted a job in New York City. He moved the family to a suburb and enrolled Averie in a nice elementary school a block

from their new home. She wouldn't need to take a bus and could sleep later since school was so close. The bus came early in Montreal, and Averie had a long ride to school.

"You need to go inside," Averie's mother said, taking her hand and tugging at it. "Your teachers will help you learn English better than I have. You will learn to write it and not just speak it."

"But, Momma, I don't want to go to school here. Please take me back to Montreal," Averie said in French.

"I know you don't want to go to school, but you must. You will have a good day once you get inside."

Averie's mother kissed her on the cheek and turned to walk away. She heard Averie sniffle but knew she had to leave.

Averie sat at her desk and watched her classmates walk into the classroom before the final bell rang. Some looked at her, and some walked past her without looking or saying anything. This made Averie feel more uncomfortable than she had been feeling. She knew she'd never make friends, and with her broken

English, she was certain she'd never have friends at her new school.

The teacher, Mr. Cardinal, called the class to attention and introduced Averie.

"Averie comes to us from Montreal, Quebec, Canada. Can anyone tell me where Canada is located?"

Luca Jamerson raised his hand. "It's above the United States," he said proudly.

"Very good," Mr. Cardinal said. "How do you know this? We haven't studied it yet, but we will this year."

"My mom is from Montreal," Luca answered. "We go there a lot to see my grandparents."

"That's wonderful. Perhaps you can show Averie around the school."

"I'd be happy to," Luca said.

"Please go now," Mr. Cardinal said. "Averie, Luca will show you the gym, cafeteria, and art and music rooms. He'll show you the restrooms and the nurse's room."

Averie stood and followed behind Luca.

"Would you be more comfortable if I spoke to you in French?" Luca asked, noticing Averie's broken English.

"You speak French?" Averie asked, surprised.

"Yes, I do. Would you like me to help you with your English? I know it's not easy to learn. I can help you during lunch. We have about twenty minutes after we eat to sit and talk. I could help you then."

"That would be nice," Averie said. She was thrilled to meet a new friend, and she wanted help with her English so she wouldn't feel out of place.

Averie and Luca walked the halls and showed Averie all the places she would need to know. They walked slowly and talked the entire time. Averie felt comfortable with Luca. He understood what it was like being in a new school and not fluent in the language.

Averie was already feeling better when she returned to the classroom. Mr. Cardinal was patient and helped her when she didn't understand something. Reading was hard for Averie because she learned to speak English but didn't spend a lot of time working on sight words and spelling.

When the lunch bell rang, Luca walked Averie to the cafeteria. He sat with her, and they conversed in French and some English. Averie was so happy to have someone who could speak her native tongue. Luca was fluent in French and English and knew little Spanish. Averie was impressed with his language skills.

"You are smart," Averie told Luca. "How did you get so smart?"

"I read a lot," he answered. "I like to read, and I don't have many friends, so I don't go to many places. How about you?"

"I have no friends here," Averie said. "I have some back home. Well, what was my home."

80

"Would you like to be my friend?" Luca asked. "I can help you learn English after school sometimes."

"Yes, I will be your friend," Averie said. "I'm not sure I'll ever learn English the way you know it."

"Sure, you will. It just takes time."

Averie and Luca started meeting at Averie's house after school every day. They would study English together and have a snack when they were finished. Luca's mother would pick him up promptly at four-thirty.

The days passed, and Averie thought she wasn't progressing with reading. She was doing better with speaking, and Luca was proud of how much better she was doing. Even Mr. Cardinal commended her for her hard work in learning a new language.

Still, she struggled with reading and writing. Averie was frustrated. She wanted to give up. She wasn't making a lot of progress, and whenever she tried to cancel the after-school study sessions, Luca wouldn't let her. Even Averie's mother wasn't letting her cancel.

"I just don't want to do this anymore," Averie cried to her mother as she was tucked into bed. Averie thought she was too old to be tucked in, but her mother insisted and would sing her a song or read her a short story in English.

"Averie, honey, we will be living here for a long time. You need to learn English so you can do well in school."

"I will move back to Montreal when I'm old enough, so I don't need to know English that well. Besides, all this time learning English will make me forget French."

"You will never forget French," her mother said. "You never forget your native language, even if you don't speak it in a long time. It's always there for you."

Averie said goodnight and asked her mother to turn out her light.

"Tomorrow will be a new day," her mother said as she left Averie's room. "Each day will bring you closer to your goal of reading and writing in English."

The next day at school, Luca didn't sit with Averie at lunch or talk to her all day. Averie didn't know why, and she wasn't too worried. She thought maybe Luca was just having a bad day. But she knew something was wrong when he didn't show up at her house for their study session.

"Why don't you call him?" Averie's mother said. "Don't be afraid to ask him what's going on."

Averie shook her head and went to her room. She wasn't going to call Luca. He could call or say something at school if she wanted to talk to her.

Three days passed with Luca not talking to Averie in school or showing up for their study session. Averie sat alone in the cafeteria and watched Luca talking and laughing with other kids. She never saw him talking to many other kids, so she was happy he found new friends but sad he was no longer hers.

After school, Averie decided to ask Luca what was going on. She waited for him to come out of the school.

"Luca, why are you mad at me?" she asked. "Did I do something wrong?"

"Averie, I've been working with you for a month, and you don't seem interested in learning to read and write in English. You're just wasting my time."

Averie started to cry. "I-I just want to live in Montreal. And the English is hard."

"Listen, Averie. Learning anything new takes perseverance. You don't have that. I'm not trying to be mean. I'm being honest."

"Per...ser... what?" she asked.

"Perseverance. It means not giving up. It means doing something even if it's hard," Luca explained.

"Perseverance," Averie said slowly. "If you come to study with me tomorrow, I will show you perseverance."

"I'll think about it," Luca said.

84

Averie walked home from school, saddened that she discouraged Luca and made him feel unappreciated. She walked into her house and saw Luca sitting in the living room with her mother.

"What are you doing here?" Averie asked.

Luca stood and smiled. "Well, I decided if you can have perseverance, so can I. Let's get started on today's lesson!"

PRACTICE MAKES PERFECT

Elena wanted nothing more than to make her school's cheerleading squad. She practiced every day in front of her bedroom mirror, making sure each move was just right.

Her mother bought her pom-poms so she could practice using them. Elena moved her bed and rearranged her dressers and

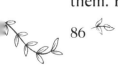

desk, so she had room to jump. She went to her backyard to do cartwheels. She didn't forget anything. She even watched videos on the internet of cheerleading squads at competitions.

Elena knew she might not make the team. It was going to be very competitive. Many girls signed up for tryouts. When she left school Friday, thirty names were on the list, and there was still a week left to sign up. That also meant one more week to practice.

Elena's best friend Susan didn't want Elena to try out.

"You won't make it because you aren't popular. Only the popular girls make it whether they're good or not," Susan said.

"I don't care. I want to try out, and if I don't make it, I'll be okay," Elena said.

"You'll be sorry and feel bad," Susan said. "You probably won't make the first cut because they want to make sure the popular girls make it."

Elena didn't understand why her best friend would discourage her from doing something she desperately wanted. She worked hard for weeks to perfect her moves. She convinced her mother to let her take gymnastics so she could learn to do the splits and cartwheels.

For a year, Elena went to gymnastics class every Saturday morning for an hour. She enjoyed it, and even if she didn't make the cheerleading squad this year, she would try again next year and the next and the next until she made it.

Elena knew Susan wasn't wholly wrong. It did seem like the popular girls were cheerleaders, and that's why she practiced so much. Practice makes perfect, her mother would tell her.

When Elena didn't understand long division, her teacher told her the more she practiced, the easier it would become. Her teacher was right. Elena practiced long division every day for two weeks, and it became easy. It was so easy she'd forgotten how she didn't understand it.

Cheerleading was the same. Elena learned by watching videos, going to her school's basketball game, and watching the cheerleaders. Sometimes, she didn't pay attention to the game at all. Her mother told her she should because it's essential to understand the game and when to cheer.

Elena started watching basketball games on television, and her brother Ben explained what was happening. Ben was a year younger, but he was a big help to Elena and knew how much she wanted to be a cheerleader. He was always ready to go outside to spot his sister when she did cartwheels.

"You got this," Ben would tell her with every perfect cartwheel. "You will make the squad. You are so good!"

Elena could only hope Ben was right. She thought about what Susan said but didn't let it bother her.

"Hey, El, I see you signed up to try out for cheerleading," Nancy said as she sat next to Elena in music class. "I don't know why you're doing it. I know I'll make it, and my friends will too."

Nancy was one of the most popular girls in middle school. She had a lot of friends, and she was on the cheer squad last year, so Elena was sure she'd be on it again. There were seven openings, and the list of girls trying out was growing.

Elena checked the list each day before leaving school. It was thirty-eight the day before tryouts, and she hoped no one else signed up. Thirty-eight are trying out for seven positions. Elena knew the odds weren't good, especially since Susan and Maria would likely make it because they were on the team last year. And Susan will probably make sure her friends make it.

Coach Sari Ford saw Elena reading the list.

"Hi, Elena. I'm Coach Sari Ford, but you can call me Coach Sari. I see you'll be trying out tomorrow. Have you ever done cheerleading?"

"It's nice to meet you, Coach Sari. I've never been on a cheer squad but have been practicing. I want to make it. It's all I've ever wanted to do."

Coach Sari smiled. "It takes a lot of practice. I wish there were more openings, but the school only allows me to have fourteen on the squad. I choose two alternates who practice with us and fill in when one of the girls is absent."

"I would be happy being an alternate if I'm not good enough yet," Elena said. "I know with so many trying out, I don't have a good chance."

"That's not the attitude to have," Coach Sari said. "Think positively; if you've practiced, you should do well."

Elena could barely sleep that night. She was so excited. She couldn't wait for tryouts.

Ben waited by the door for his sister so they could walk to school together. Along the way, he gave her a pep talk.

"Remember, sis, you can do this. Just don't get all nervous and jittery. Stay calm and remember what you've been practicing."

"I will, Ben. I'm not nervous. I'm more excited than anything. I can't wait for the school day to end. It's going to feel like forever waiting for tryouts to start."

Susan sat with Elena at lunch and tried to talk Elena out of trying out.

"Why are you doing this?" Elena asked. "Why don't you want me to try out?"

"I just don't want you to be disappointed," Susan answered. "Cheerleading is for the popular girls. You should try out for track. You run fast, and almost everyone makes the team."

"Well, you have no confidence in me," Elena said. "You're supposed to be my friend and give me encouragement."

Susan pushed her broccoli around with her fork. "I can't stand broccoli. Why do they give it to us?"

Elena sighed. "You're changing the subject, but that's okay. I guess you aren't a true friend. I don't like broccoli either, but it has nothing to do with your lack of confidence in me."

"Sorry," Susan said. She picked up her tray, stood, and walked away.

Elena didn't understand why her friend acted that way but didn't have time to worry about it.

The bell rang, signaling the end of the school day. Elena walked as fast as she could to the gym. When she arrived, she was surprised to see Susan.

"Why are you here?" Elena asked her friend.

"Why do you think? I'm trying out."

"But your name isn't on the list."

"Look again," Susan said, pointing. "I talked to the coach, and she said it was okay for me to try out."

Just then, Coach Sari called to the girls to line up.

"We're going to start with voices. I'll go down the line, and you need to shout, 'Go, team, go. Win tonight,' when I point to you. At the end, I will call the names of those who made this cut."

As Coach went down the line, everyone shouted and made the cut. Next, they had to do a short cheer with their pom-poms. Three girls were eliminated, two never showed, and one girl had scratched her name off the list, so thirty-three girls were left.

The coach had them perform drill after drill, dropping the number even more as some were eliminated.

With only twenty girls left, it was time to do cartwheels, high jumps, and splits.

Elena was confident she did well. She left feeling good because she did her best. The coach said she would post the names of those who made it the following day by noon. That gave Elena plenty of time to check before she went to the cafeteria for lunch.

She didn't need to wait for lunch. Nancy sat next to her in music class.

"Congratulations, I see you made the team."

"How do you know?" Elena asked.

"The list is posted. I just saw it on the way here. You made it. I didn't," she said.

"Wait, what do you mean you didn't make it?" Elena was surprised.

"I guess I was too confident. I thought if I were in the squad last year, I'd be on it automatically this year, but that's not how it works, and I didn't practice at all," Nancy said, tears forming in her eyes.

"I don't know what to say," Elena said. "I'm so sorry."

"Your friend Susan made the team too. You're a lucky girl," Nancy said.

Later, when Elena said Susan, she congratulated her.

"I'm happy for you, but I don't understand why you didn't want me to try out," Elena said.

"You practiced so much every day. I was afraid I wouldn't make it if I had to compete against you," Susan said. "I'm sorry. It was wrong of me. I practiced every day, too, and I didn't tell you."

"It's okay," Elena said. "We both made it. That's all that matters."

Susan hugged her friend. "I guess for both of us, practice made perfect."

A LISTENING EAR

Ring! Ring! Ring!

"Ugh!" came a loud groan. Slowly, the mound of blankets moved, and a thin, pale arm slithered from underneath. Contrary to its frail appearance, the arm slammed the alarm into complete silence.

Peace had been achieved.

It wasn't ten minutes later when Stacy toppled the blankets she had been buried under—an expression of utter horror hijacking her face.

"I'm late!" she screamed.

Granted, sleeping in could be listed as Stacy's most loved hobby; she hated it right now. In an extreme panic, Stacy pulled clothes from her wardrobe, not caring if they paired well.

She got ready in record time and flew to the kitchen. Yet, instead of the aroma of freshly baked pancakes, what greeted her was the fragrance of dish soap. The kitchen held none of its usual warmth because the person who gave life to it was missing. Stacie found a note from her mother on the kitchen counter, next to a Pop-Tart.

Honey,

I had to go to work early this morning. I'm sorry for not meeting you for breakfast, but I promise to make it up to you later.

Love,

Mom

Stacy sighed. She didn't like eating Pop-Tarts for breakfast; they just never felt enough. Yet, she had no choice today.

Stacy ran out of the house at top speed, munching on the Pop-Tart as she made her way to the bus stop. It seemed lady luck had simply abandoned her this morning. Stacy was just a half mile from the bus stop when she saw the last student climb onto the school bus. The door to the bus closed, and the bus driver drove off.

"No, no, no!" Stacy cried. "Stop!"

It was no use; the bus had already left. Not only would she be late for school, but walking all the way meant she would miss most of the first period, too. Her first lesson was English, a subject she was good at. All weekend, she had worked on writing the perfect piece of fiction. A masterpiece she had been waiting to show to her teacher. Now, she wouldn't be able to.

Half of the first lesson had passed by the time she reached school. As she entered class, she could feel the scrutinizing gaze of her classmates poking into her back. The most painful reaction was that of Mrs. Johnson. She looked disappointed. An expression that had never been directed at Stacy.

Stacy didn't get the opportunity to explain herself. Mrs. Johnson wordlessly extended the tardy slip to her. Stacy felt so embarrassed she could barely mutter an apology before she left to take her seat.

For Stacy, things just got worse and worse.

The next lesson was math. A subject Stacy didn't excel at. Just doing a normal classwork exercise was a chore, but today, it came with a bomb. Their teacher, Mr. Peter, had taken a pop quiz last week.

As he gave the day's assignment to them, he announced, "I've checked your quizzes and will distribute them shortly."

Stacy knew he hadn't done well on the quiz. Yet, when Mr. Peter slapped her quiz paper on her desk, a shocked gasp escaped her lips.

"This can't be?!" Stacy said in disbelief as she stared at the giant red "F" on her paper.

She had failed.

"Ms. Stacy," Mr. Johnson called. "Can I please have a word?" He said as he sat back at his desk.

As Stacy shuffled to the front of the class, she knew what Mr. Peter would say.

"Ms. Stacy, I'm very disappointed with your performance," he said.

At that moment, Stacy wanted to burst into tears. Her day hadn't started well; she didn't get to enjoy her favorite subject, and now she had failed math. She had never failed a subject, ever. Before Mr. Peter could say anything more, the bell rang, signaling the end of the period.

As the tide of students flooded out of the class, Stacy allowed herself to be pushed out with them—anything to save herself from further embarrassment.

It was finally Stacy's lunch period. She needed to let out the emotions swirling inside of her. And what better way to do that than to talk to her best friends?

Even that didn't go as planned.

"…and then she called Jake," Sylvie went on.

"I…" Stacy had just started to say something when she was cut off.

"We have to tell Tracy," Maria commented.

"I …" Stacy tried again.

And again

And again.

But somehow, her friends always ignored her voice. It seemed they were just so busy with their own stories and problems that they didn't care to know what was happening with her.

"I can't stay here," Stacy thought.

More than anything she had faced that day, it hurt that none of her friends had time for her. Stacy could feel tears pooling in her eyes. She couldn't take the embarrassment of being a crybaby, not after the awful day she had.

Silently, Stacy got up and left the cafeteria. She found a secluded corner in the school garden. That's when the floodgates opened. She cried and cried and cried.

Through her tears, she failed to notice someone passing by.

"Hey," a voice called out. "Are you okay?".

Stacy blinked through the flood of tears to see who it was. She saw ruffled blond hair, a freckled face, and brown eyes hidden behind round spectacles. It was none other than Tom McKay.

Tom was a boy in Stacy's science class. Although they had been studying together for almost a year, this was the first time he talked to her. Tom was a brilliant student who always sat in front of the class and answered all the teacher's questions. If he weren't in class, you'd probably find him working on one of his numerous experiments in the lab. Stacy was the total opposite. She was more of a social butterfly who loved organizing and being part of significant school events.

"Is everything all right?" Tom repeated his question as Stacy continued to stare at him silently.

Stacy quickly wiped her eyes. "I'm fine; it's just my pollen allergy acting up."

Tom blinked at her, not believing a word. "That's one wild allergy you have." He sat beside her and asked again, "For real, what's wrong? You can tell me; maybe I can help you?"

His expression was so sincere that Stacy felt like pouring out all her problems to him for a moment. But then, the doubts crept in.

What if he laughs at my problems?

What if he thinks I'm just being silly?

The list of "What ifs" was never-ending. But, for some reason, Stacy wanted to free herself of doubts. So, without thinking, she told Tom everything. At first, Stacy felt like crying again as she relived the painful events of the day. Yet, as she continued speaking, she felt lighter and lighter.

A heavy weight pressing down on her soul, crushing her spirit under it, started to lift.

Tom carefully listened to all Stacy had to say, not interrupting her.

"That's horrible," Tom said. "I wish I could've helped you."

As Tom said those words, Stacy realized something. Tom was wrong. He had already helped her in the best way possible.

"You already have," Stacy replied with a soft smile. "Sometimes all a person needs is a listening ear."

EPILOGUE

-cue the drum roll-

Celebrations are in order because you, my champion, have completed one milestone in our journey. You've finished this book.

By now, I sincerely hope each of these stories has helped you grow and helped to remind you of a fact I always knew to be true: you are Awesome!

Through the tales of each girl in this book, I hope you'll see that you are never alone in your struggles. And no matter how tough times are, YOU can make your way out. And as you shine at your brightest, in the darkest hours, you become a ray of hope for all those around you.

At the end of this book, if there is one thing I'd like to say, it's that I know you have the power to do it all. You can be the hero of your own story. And know I will be cheering for you every

step of the way. Know that I am proud of who you are. Maybe one day, you'll want to share your story with the rest of the world, too.

Until then, thank you for becoming a part of this book! Your next milestone will be to become your own hero. I'll be cheering for you, supergirl!

Your biggest fan and supporter

Michelle

REVIEW

As a children's book author, it would not only be a great help but also a joy for me if you could leave an honest review on Amazon.

I believe that these types of books play a crucial role in nurturing children's character, boosting their self-confidence, enhancing their relationships with friends and family, and encouraging them to be the best version of themselves, all while bringing them happiness.

I hope we can share many more stories together!

Here's the QR code for the review. Choose the marketplace of your preferred country!

Amazon US review

Amazon UK review

Amazon Canada review

Printed in Great Britain
by Amazon

51262460R00063